How do I catch a fish?

Contents

Written by Sally Morgan

Illustrated by Ángeles Peinador

Collins

T0321638

What's in this book?

Listen and say

pot

crab

net

shrimps

Download the audio at www.collins.co.uk/839757

rod

trawler

Chapter 1 Fish around the world

All around the world, people work hard
to catch fish to eat. Some people catch fish
in rivers. Some people go out to sea in boats.

Here are some of the fish that they catch.
Which fish do you like to eat?

salmon

carp

sea bream

mackerel

red snapper

cod

tilapia

catfish

7

Let's look at a fish. Fish don't have arms and legs like us. They have fins. How many fins can you count on this fish?

There are scales all over the body.

Fish also have gills so they can **breathe** in water.

tail

fin

eye

scales

gill

mouth

We don't only eat fish from the oceans and rivers. Crabs and shrimps aren't fish. They have a **hard** shell and ten legs. Sometimes we call them **shellfish**.

Can you see how they are different from fish?

crab

shell

shrimp

Chapter 2 Where do fish live?

You can find fish all around the world in lakes, rivers, and oceans.

About half of the fish live in the ocean.

Some fish live at the bottom of the ocean, where it's **dark** all the time.

Some fish live in very cold water and sometimes under ice.

Chapter 3 Fishing around the world

People in different places catch fish in different ways.

On the Amazon River in South America, people use spears to catch fish. A spear is a long stick with a **pointed** end.

To use the spear, you stand very quietly in the water or on a boat and you don't move, so the fish don't see you. When a fish swims near you, throw the spear at it. It takes a lot of practice to be good at spear fishing.

spear

Would you like to try spear fishing?
Would you be good at it?

In the Arctic, it's very cold in the winter. There is ice on top of the lakes and rivers, but people still catch fish.

People put on **thick** clothes and then they walk onto the ice. They make a **hole** in the ice. Then they drop a line and hook into the hole and wait for a fish.

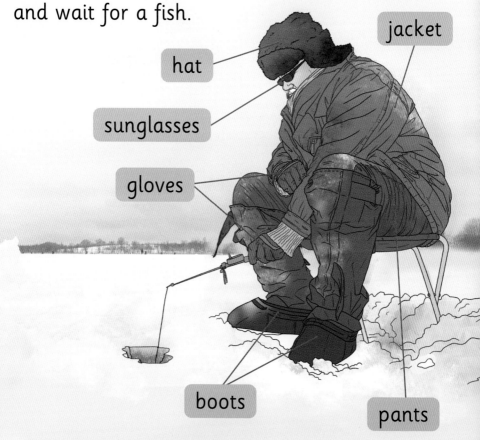

jacket

hat

sunglasses

gloves

boots

pants

In India, people use nets to catch fish in rivers. They learn to throw the net when they are young.

To catch a fish, you walk into the water and wait. When you see a fish in the water, you throw the net onto the water. Can you see how they do this?

Now the fish are in the net. You pull the net out of the water and catch the fish.

net

In China, people **trap** fish in small **pots**.
The pots come in many shapes.

To catch the fish, you put some food inside
the pot. Then you sail down the river and drop
your pot onto the bottom of the river. The fish
want the food and go into the pot, but they
can't swim out.

The next day, you pull the pot out of the water and see what is inside.

A **trawler** is a large boat that pulls a very big fishing net called a trawl. These fishing boats catch many fish.

Trawlers sail out to sea. The fishermen drop the net into the water behind the boat.
The boat pulls the net through the water.
Can you see the net in the water?

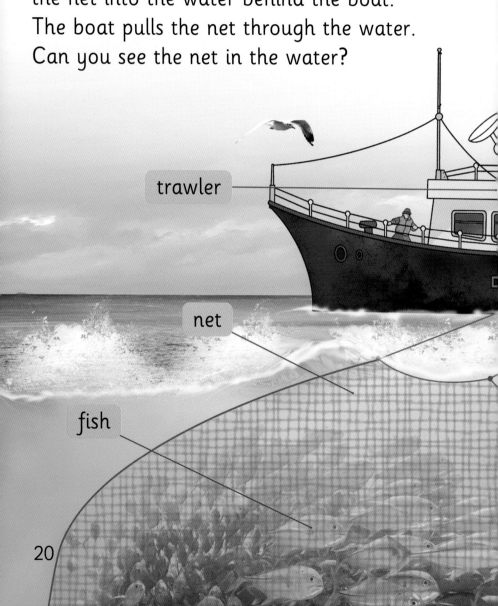

trawler

net

fish

The net catches a lot of fish, then they pull the net onto the boat.

Some trawlers are at sea for many weeks.
The trawler goes up and down in the ocean.
It's often very cold and wet on the trawler.

The fishermen wear thick jackets and pants to stay dry.

It's a very difficult job.

Chapter 4 Fishing as a hobby

Many people enjoy fishing. It's their hobby.

These people are fishing by the ocean. They have a fishing rod and line to catch fish.

What do you do to catch a fish?

First, put some food on the hook. Then drop the hook in the water with your rod. Fish see the food in the water and eat it. The hook catches a fish.

hook

When the rod moves, you pull the fish out of the water.

Fish are not easy to hold. Don't let it go!

rod

line

Rock pools are pools of water between the rocks. They are home to crabs and small fish. Can you see the crab hiding under the rock?

You can catch a crab with a rod and line. Put some meat on the end of the line and drop it into the pool. When the crab takes the meat, pull the line out of the water.

claw

leg

Be careful! Crabs have big claws. They can hurt your **fingers**!

Always leave the crab in the water.

You can make a small fish **trap** from a **plastic** bottle. This fish trap catches small fish like minnows. Minnows live in streams, rivers, and lakes.

Put some bread in the trap. Then put the trap in the water. Let it fall to the bottom.

The minnows see the bread and swim inside the trap.

minnows

Chapter 5 Be careful!

Don't catch too many fish!

Fish is very good for you. People eat it all around the world.

Other animals – like dolphins, sharks, and penguins – eat fish, too. They want a lot of fish like us.

It's important that we don't catch too many fish. Leave small fish in the rivers and oceans so they can grow and have baby fish.

That is best for everyone.

Mini-dictionary

Listen and read

breathe (verb) When a person or animal **breathes**, they take air into their body and let it out again.

dark (adjective) A **dark** place has very little light in it, or no light at all.

finger (noun) Your **finger** is one of the long thin parts at the end of your hand.

hard (adjective) Something that is **hard** is not easily bent, cut, or broken.

hole (noun) A **hole** in something is a part of it that is open.

plastic (adjective) Something that is **plastic** is made of a light, strong, material that is made by humans.

pointed (adjective) Something that is **pointed** has a sharp part at one end.

pot (noun) A **pot** is an object that is used to try to catch fish.

shellfish (noun) **Shellfish** are small animals that live in the ocean and have a shell.

thick (adjective) **Thick** clothes are heavy so that they keep you warm.

trap (noun) A **trap** is something that is used to catch animals or fish.

trap (verb) If you **trap** animals or fish, you catch them in a trap.

trawler (noun) A **trawler** is a boat used for fishing.

1 Look and match

pot fishing

net fishing

Arctic fishing

spear fishing

2 Listen and say

Collins

Published by Collins
An imprint of HarperCollins*Publishers*
Westerhill Road
Bishopbriggs
Glasgow
G64 2QT

HarperCollins*Publishers*
1st Floor, Watermarque Building
Ringsend Road
Dublin 4
Ireland

William Collins' dream of knowledge for all began with the publication of his first book in 1819.

A self-educated mill worker, he not only enriched millions of lives, but also founded a flourishing publishing house. Today, staying true to this spirit, Collins books are packed with inspiration, innovation, and practical expertise. They place you at the center of a world of possibility and give you exactly what you need to explore it.

© HarperCollins*Publishers* Limited 2020

10 9 8 7 6 5 4 3 2

ISBN 978-0-00-839757-9

Collins® and COBUILD® are registered trademarks of HarperCollins*Publishers* Limited

www.collins.co.uk/elt

British Library Cataloguing in Publication Data

A catalogue record for this publication is available from the British Library.

Author: Sally Morgan
Illustrator: Ángeles Peinador (Beehive)
Series editor: Rebecca Adlard
Publishing manager: Lisa Todd
Product managers: Jennifer Hall and Caroline Green
In-house editor: Alma Puts Keren
Project manager: Emily Hooton
Editor: Matthew Hancock
Proofreaders: Natalie Murray and Michael Lamb
Cover designer: Kevin Robbins
Typesetter: 2Hoots Publishing Services Ltd
Audio produced by id audio, London
Reading guide author: Emma Wilkinson
Production controller: Rachel Weaver
Printed and bound by: GPS Group, Slovenia

MIX
Paper from
responsible sources

FSC
www.fsc.org

FSC™ C007454

Download the audio for this book and a reading guide for parents and teachers at www.collins.co.uk/839757